# A car f



Winky is the only one I know who can understand my squeaks, because he's a hamster, too.

"Glad you could visit, Humph," Winky said. "Wait until you see my wheels."

I looked closely at Winky. He had four paws, just like me. I didn't see any wheels.

"What wheels?" I asked.

"On my car," he said. "The Paynes got me my very own car."

I had a lovely big cage, a wheel for spinning and a hamster ball.

But I *didn't* have a car.

# Humphrey's
## Really Wheely Racing Day

HUMPHREY'S TINY TALES

**Betty G. Birney**

*illustrated by* **Priscilla Burris**

SCHOLASTIC INC.

ISBN 978-1-338-04737-0



12 11 10 9 8 7 6 5 4 3 2 16 17 18 19 20 21

Printed in the U.S.A. 40

First Scholastic printing, March 2016

Design by Ryan Thomann

*To Anna and Tobias Ross*

*—B.B.*

*To SWEET-SWEET-SWEET Betty Birney—*

*thank you for Humphrey!*

*—P.B.*

# Contents

# A Wheely Great Weekend

It was Friday afternoon in Room 26 of Longfellow School. I was spinning on my hamster wheel, trying to stay calm.

Fridays are always exciting for me.

Every Friday afternoon, I get to go home for the weekend with a different classmate.

It's the BEST-BEST-BEST part of my job as classroom pet.

Of course, Mrs. Brisbane knew whose turn it was to bring me home. She plans my visits with the parents.

But sometimes she forgets to tell *me*.

Who would it be this week?

Would it be Lower-Your-Voice-A.J., whose whole family likes to talk loudly?

Or would I go to Speak-Up-Sayeh's house, where everyone speaks quietly?

"Mrs. Brisbane, who is taking Humphrey home?" Heidi Hopper asked.

"Raise-Your-Hand-Heidi," Mrs. Brisbane told her. Heidi forgets to raise her hand a lot.

Mandy Payne said, "I am!"

She forgot to raise her hand, too!

Then Mandy said, "That clock must be stuck. It's taking forever to get to the end of the day."

Don't-Complain-Mandy Payne used to complain about a lot of things.

Ever since she got her own

hamster, named Winky, she doesn't complain as much.

"I can't wait!" I shouted.

My friends giggled, even though all they heard me say was "SQUEAK-SQUEAK-SQUEAK!"

Just then, the clock hand

moved and the bell rang. The end of the day had finally come!

My friend Og the frog splashed loudly in his tank.

He's a classroom pet, too. He doesn't go home with students on the weekend because he doesn't have to eat every day, like I do.

"I'll tell you all about my weekend at Mandy's when I get back," I squeaked.

"BOING-BOING-BOING!" he replied, hopping up and down.

He makes a funny sound because he's a funny frog.

Soon Mandy's mom arrived to pick us up.

"Humphwee!" a tiny voice shouted.

It was Mandy's little brother.

"Hi, Bwian," I squeaked back. His name is "Brian," but he calls himself "Bwian."

Mandy's two younger sisters, Pammy and Tammy, rushed up to my cage. The girls are twins, but they don't look anything alike.

"*I'm* going to take care of you, Humphrey," Pammy said.

"No, *I'm* going to take care of you, Humphrey," Tammy said.

"You're both wrong," Mandy said. "*I'm* going to take care of Humphrey, because he's *my* classroom pet."

When we got to their house, Mandy put me on a table in the living room next to Winky's cage!

"Hi, Humphrey!" Winky said.

When Winky was born, one of his eyes didn't open, so he always looks like he's winking.

"Hi, Winky!" I replied. "How are things going?"

"Everything is hamster-iffic with me," he squeaked.

"Same with me," I said.

Winky is the only one I know who can understand my squeaks, because he's a hamster, too.

"Glad you could visit, Humph," Winky said. "Wait until you see my wheels."

I looked closely at Winky. He had four paws, just like me. I didn't see any wheels.

"What wheels?" I asked.

"On my car," he said. "The Paynes got me my very own car."

I had a lovely big cage, a wheel for spinning and a hamster ball.

But I *didn't* have a car.

"Look at them. I think they're talking," Mandy squealed.

Tammy, Pammy and Bwian—I mean Brian—all giggled.

"I wonder what they are talking about?" Mandy said. "Oh, I know! Humphrey wants to see Winky's car!"

Mandy put a hamster-sized car on the floor.

It was bright blue and it had four wheels. In the middle was a bigger wheel, like the wheel I spin on.

This was one really wheely car!

"It's wonderful!" I said.

"Watch this!" Mandy put Winky in the big wheel and he started spinning. As the wheel spun, the car began to roll.

Mandy took me out of my cage and held me in her hand so I could watch.

"Go, Winky!"

I squeaked.

"Go, Winky, go!" Pammy, Tammy and Brian shouted.

Winky made the wheel go faster and faster.

Zoom! The car glided across the room.

When it got to the other side, Tammy picked the car up and turned it around.

Zoom! The car glided across the room in the other direction.

"Keep going, Winky!" Mandy shouted.

I think I have a wonderful life as the classroom pet in Room 26. I think it's the best life a hamster ever had.

But I have to admit, I was a

TINY-TINY-TINY bit jealous of Winky.

I wanted a really wheely car, too!

After a while, Mandy put me back in my cage. Then she stopped the car and took Winky out.

"I don't want you to get tired," she said as she put him back in the cage.

"Thanks, Mandy!" he squeaked.

Of course, I was the only one who could understand him.

"Do you mind sharing?" she asked Winky.

Winky squeaked, "Not at all."

Before I could squeak "Thanks," Mandy put *me* in the car.

The car felt a lot like my nice yellow hamster ball. But this was no everyday hamster ball. This was a really wheely car!

I started spinning on the wheel.

Zoom! The car lurched forward.

Zoom! I spun faster and the car rolled across the room.

I spun faster and faster. Zoom! Zoom!

"Go,
Humphrey,
go!"
Mandy shouted.

"Go, go, go," Pammy, Tammy and Brian shouted.

I was going so fast, they couldn't keep up.

BAM! The car slammed into the wall. It spun around and rolled in the other direction.

"Isn't it fun?" Winky squeaked.

"It's the most fun I've ever had!" I shouted.

ZOOM-ZOOM-ZOOM!

I could have driven that car forever.

For the rest of the weekend, Winky and I took turns racing the bright blue car.

One time, Mandy put me in my hamster ball so Winky and I could roll along next to each other. We whizzed through the dining room and into the kitchen.

It was fun, but my hamster ball doesn't have wheels.

"If you had a car, we could have a *real* race," Winky said.

"I hope I'll have a really

wheely car of my own someday," I told him.

"I hope so, too, Humphrey," Winky said with a wink. "I really do."

# ZOOM-ZOOM-ZOOM Around the Room

When I got back to Room 26 on Monday, I told Og about the car right away.

"There was a car and it was blue and I went ZOOM-ZOOM-ZOOM!" I squeaked.

"BOING-BOING-BOING-BOING!" Og jumped up and down in his tank.

"I'll tell you the rest later," I said.

The bell rang and class began.

Before our math lesson, Mrs. Brisbane asked Mandy to tell us about our weekend.

"We had so much fun," Mandy said. "I think Humphrey and Winky were happy to see each other. At least they squeaked a lot."

All my friends giggled. Stop-Giggling-Gail laughed the loudest.

"And Humphrey really loved rolling around in Winky's hamster car," she explained.

"Car?" A.J. said in his loud voice. "He has a *car*?"

Mandy nodded. "Yes. It looks like a car, but it has a hamster wheel in the middle. Humphrey loved it as much as Winky does."

"I never saw a hamster car," Pay-Attention-Art said.

"Me either," Heidi added.

"Well, Humphrey liked it so much that I brought it with me to school," Mandy said. "Is it all right to show them, Mrs. Brisbane?"

Mrs. Brisbane smiled. "Of course, Mandy. I'd like to see it, too."

Mandy reached in her backpack and there it was. The little blue car!

"Oooh," my classmates said.

"Ahhh," Mrs. Brisbane said. "Why don't you show us how it works?"

Mandy gently took me out of my cage and put me in the racing car. She set the car on the floor and I began to spin the wheel.

"Go, Humphrey, go!" Richie shouted as I rolled the car between the students' tables.

I spun the wheel a little faster.

"Faster, Humphrey, faster!" I heard A.J. shout.

"BOING-BOING-BOING!" Og yelled as he splashed in the water side of his tank.

My friends all stood up to watch me, so I spun even faster.

Uh-oh. Wait-for-the-Bell-Garth's foot was in the aisle.

There was no way for me to stop the car and I didn't have a steering wheel. I leaned to the right and the car barely missed his foot.

"I hope he doesn't lose control," Mrs. Brisbane said.

It wasn't easy, but I kept the car going without rolling *into* something.

"Humphrey! Humphrey! Humphrey!" my classmates chanted.

All their cheering made me spin even faster.

Before I knew it, my car rolled up against the leg of Mrs. Brisbane's desk.

The car bounced backward, went into a spin and suddenly stopped . . . like THAT!

Mrs. Brisbane had stopped the car with her foot.

"Humphrey, I think you need a rest," she said.

I had to admit she was right.

Mrs. Brisbane put me in my cage. "I can see that Humphrey

had a great time at your house," she told Mandy.

"Yes," Mandy replied. "I put Humphrey in his hamster ball and Winky in the car and they raced each other," she said. "But I think Humphrey would like his own car. Then they could have a *real* race."

"A hamster race!" Garth said. "I'd like to see that!"

"Humphrey should have his own car," Golden-Miranda said.

"That's right!" A.J. said in that LOUD-LOUD-LOUD voice of his.

"They could race,
and I know Humphrey-Dumpty would win!"

I like the funny nickname A.J. calls me.

"Thanks!" I squeaked.

"BOING-BOING!" Og said.

When I looked around, all my classmates were smiling.

"Winky might win. He knows how to make his car go really fast," Mandy said. "But the car costs a lot of money. I got Winky's car for my birthday."

Money! Sometimes I forget about human things, like money.

My friends weren't smiling anymore.

"Maybe we can find a way. Let me think about it," Mrs. Brisbane said. "Now it's time to start math."

It wasn't easy for me to think about math after all that excitement.

When Mrs. Brisbane wrote an "8" on the board, it looked like a race track with fun twists and turns.

While my friends studied science, Mrs. Brisbane put me in the car and let me roll around Room 26.

Whenever I got close to a wall, a classmate helped turn the car around.

It was fun, but not as much fun as being in my own car and racing Winky would be.

Mandy got her car back at the end of the day.

"I'm sure Winky will want this," Mrs. Brisbane said.

"Yes," Mandy said. "But I hope Humphrey gets a car, too."

"YES-YES-YES!" I squeaked.

"BOING-BOING-BOING!" Og took a big leap into the water side of his tank.

Mandy giggled. "I forgot about Og. I wonder if they have frog cars."

"Now, that would be funny!" Mrs. Brisbane said with a smile.

Later that evening, Og and I were alone. I opened the lock-that-doesn't-lock on my cage and walked over to Og's tank.

"Do you want to be in a race?" I asked.

"BOING." Og didn't sound very sure.

"Well, I do," I said. "And if there's a car for hamsters, there should be a car for frogs, too."

"BOING-BOING!" Og seemed more interested.

I tried to picture Og driving a car. With his big webbed feet, I

didn't see how he could spin the wheel to make it go.

"Don't be upset," I told him. "I don't have a car, either."

Og and I were quiet for the rest of the evening.

At least I could pretend to have a really wheely car, even if it wasn't the same at all.

# Really Wheely and Red

The next morning, Mrs. Brisbane entered Room 26 with a big smile on her face and a large box in her hand. She said, "Last night, I went to Pet-O-Rama."

Pet-O-Rama? That's the pet shop where I used to live!

"I told the manager we want to have a hamster car race to go along with our math unit on measurement," Mrs. Brisbane explained. "And he wants to help us."

The manager—my old friend, Carl—wanted to help?

"YIPPEE-YIPPEE-YIPPEE!" I squeaked.

My friends looked as happy as I was.

The door opened and Mr. Morales, the head of Longfellow School, walked in.

"Good morning, class," he said. He turned to Mrs. Brisbane. "What did you want to show me?"

"This," our teacher said.

She opened the box and reached in.

She took out a car.

It wasn't a real car. It was a really wheely hamster car!

*And* it was bright red with a lightning bolt on the side!

"Eeek!" I squeaked. "It's just what I wanted."

Mrs. Brisbane told Mr. Morales about Winky's car and the idea about a hamster race. "Pet-O-Rama is giving this car to Humphrey so we can use it for math," she said.

I was so surprised, my whiskers wiggled and my tail twitched.

"It has the pet shop name on it," she said.

I scrambled to the tippy top of my cage to get a better look.

It was true. "Pet-O-Rama" was written on the back of the red racing car.

"Pet-O-Rama will also donate prizes for the winner," she said.

I LIKED-LIKED-LIKED that idea!

"I'd like to see a hamster race myself," Mr. Morales said.

"BOING!" my neighbor agreed.

"Og!" Mr. Morales said. "What do you think of a hamster race?"

Og bounced up and down in his tank. "BOING-BOING-BOING!" he said.

"We should have a frog race, too," Mr. Morales said. "But I don't think they have cars for frogs."

"Sorry, Og," I squeaked to my friend.

"We'll make our plans tomorrow," Mrs. Brisbane said. "Time to put this away."

She took the red car and put it on the bookcase.

Luckily, it was the bottom shelf! Because there was no way I could reach it on the *top* shelf.

I started thinking about a plan for later.

That night, when Aldo the custodian came in to clean, he

had a big smile on his face. Of course, Aldo always has a big smile each night he comes to Room 26.

He pushed his cleaning trolley into the room.

"Hey, buddy, have a treat," he said. He poked a tiny carrot stick into my cage.

He dropped a Froggy Fish Stick into Og's tank. Yuck!

"I heard the news about a racing day," Aldo said.

"BOING," Og chimed in.

Aldo began to sweep the floor.

"That's one race I'm not going to miss," he said. "After all, I have to cheer for my buddy."

"Thanks, Aldo!" I squeaked.

I LOVE-LOVE-LOVE it when Aldo comes to clean. But I have to admit, I was happy when he left that night.

As soon as he was gone, I jiggled the lock on my cage. I call it the lock-that-doesn't-lock because I know how to get it open.

The door opened wide and I scurried across the table.

"I'm going to try to go for a ride, Og," I squeaked.

I slid down the leg

of the table and ran across the floor to the bookcase.

There it was. The bright shiny red car!

I pulled myself up onto the bottom shelf of the bookcase. I gave the car a little push. It rolled off the shelf and hit the floor with a BUMP.

Then it ROLLED-ROLLED-ROLLED across the floor.

"Wait for me!" I shouted. I hopped off the shelf and followed the car.

The car rolled between the tables in Room 26.

"Stop!" I squeaked.

"BOING-BOING!" Og sounded worried.

Just then, the car hit the leg of A.J.'s chair and it stopped.

"Thank you," I said.

I stood up on my tippy toes

and popped the door open. Then I climbed inside.

"Here goes, Og!" I squeaked.

I began to spin the wheel. The car started slowly.

Then I spun the wheel faster. And faster.

The car zoomed across the room.

“BOING-BOING-BOING!” Og cheered.

I thought about Winky racing next to me in his blue car, so I spun even faster.

Suddenly, I looked up and saw the wall coming closer and closer.

“Eeek!” I squeaked. I stopped spinning, but the car kept on going until—BUMP! It hit the wall and stopped.

“BOING-BOING-BOING!” Og leaped up really high!

I climbed out of the car. “I’m fine, Og,” I told him. “But I don’t think I can drive the car out of the corner. And there's no human to turn it around."

"BOING!" Og leaped into the water side of his tank and started splashing.

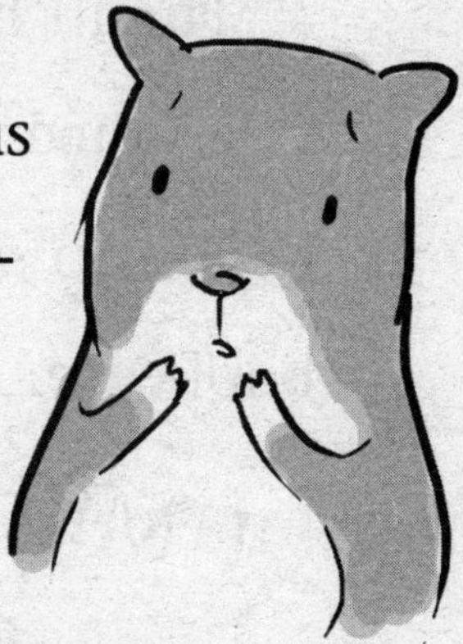

I have to admit, I was WORRIED-WORRIED-WORRIED.

Wouldn't Mrs. Brisbane wonder how the car ended up in the corner? What if she couldn't find it the next morning? Would she call off the race?

What if she found out that my lock doesn't lock . . . and then had it fixed?

I could never get out and have an adventure again!

Then I had a good idea.

I squeezed into the corner and began to *push* the car toward the bookcase.

I tried, but it was hard to move the car that way.

I pushed for a while. Then I rested for a while.

I pushed and rested for the rest of the night.

When I finally got the car to the bookcase, sunlight was peeking through the window.

Of course, I couldn't lift it up onto the shelf, but at least it was nearby.

I scurried across the floor to the table. I used the cord from the blinds to swing myself back UP-UP-UP to the table top.

"That was fun!" I squeaked as I raced past Og's tank.

"BOING-BOING!" Og said.

I pulled the cage door shut behind me and went into my sleeping hut.

I was so tired, I slept through math, reading *and* science. After all, I'd had a LONG-LONG-LONG night.

Right when I woke up, I heard

Mrs. Brisbane say, "Class, the great hamster race will be this Friday."

"Eeek!" I squeaked.

"You heard me, Humphrey," Mrs. Brisbane said. "You'd better practice."

She went over to the bookcase to get my really wheely car.

"What's it doing on the floor?" she asked. "Maybe it rolled out when Aldo was cleaning last night."

Whew! My lock-that-doesn't-lock was safe!

# A Wheely Big Day

For the next few days, Mrs. Brisbane let me practice racing my car around Room 26 while my friends took spelling tests and learned about measuring.

One afternoon, they made little banners on sticks.

"We can wave them to cheer Humphrey and Winky on," Mrs. Brisbane explained.

"I let Winky ride his car every night," Mandy said.

"Good," I squeaked. "May the best hamster win."

As soon as I said it, I realized that in the end, Winky might end up winning.

But at least I'd give the race my *best*.

Friday was a very surprising day!

First, Mandy arrived at school with Winky. She put his cage on the table by the window next to mine.

Winky had never been to school before.

After sitting through the morning lessons, Winky told Og and me that he thought being a classroom pet was wonderful.

"But I still love being Mandy's hamster," he said.

Of course he did!

After lunch, Mrs. Brisbane announced that the race was about to begin.

The whole class lined up and went out into the big hallway.

Mandy carried Winky's cage. Miranda carried my cage.

"What about Og? He'll feel left out," A.J. said.

"No, he won't," Mrs. Brisbane said. "I have a surprise for Og."

A surprise for Og? What could it be?

Some of the other classes from Longfellow School were already lined up on both sides of the hallway.

Down the middle, rows of wooden blocks divided the lanes.

There were two red lines taped to the floor.

One line was marked "Start." The other line was marked "Finish."

Some of the students had stopwatches, rulers and note-books.

I am not sure what they were going to do, but they looked excited about the race.

Mr. Morales stood by the line marked "Finish." He wore a tie with little race cars on it.

"Students, the great hamster race is about to begin," he said.

My classmates cheered and waved their banners.

"Here you go, Humphrey," Mrs. Brisbane said as she put me in my really wheely car. She closed the top and set the car on the start line.

Mandy put Winky in his blue car and set it next to mine.

"Good luck, pal!"

I squeaked.

"Same to you, Humph!"

Winky replied.

Mr. Morales said, "Ready, set, go!"

Mrs. Brisbane gave both cars a gentle push.

I didn't waste any time in getting the wheel spinning. I kept my eyes straight ahead as I spun faster and faster.

"Go, Humphrey, go!" the students called.

"Roll, Wink, roll!" they cheered.

I looked back at Winky's lane. I was ahead, but Winky's car wasn't far behind me.

I spun my wheel even faster.

And then a terrible thing happened.

I was spinning as fast as I could, but my really wheely car wasn't moving!

It had rolled up against a wooden block.

I was stuck!

I heard people moaning, "Oh, no, Humphrey!"

I heard the crowd shout, "Go, Winky! There's the finish line!"

Winky was going to win.

I spun and spun, but the car didn't budge, so I did the only thing I could think of. I reached up and pushed the lid of the car as hard as I could.

Success! The top opened and I crawled out of the car.

Maybe I couldn't win the race in my car, but I could still cross the line first!

The cheering got louder and louder.

As I raced for the finish line, I saw the banners waving above me.

I glanced up over the wooden blocks. Winky's blue car was just inches ahead of me. I ran and ran as fast as my paws could carry me and I passed the blue car!

The finish line was right in front of me, so I sprinted across it.

Winky's blue car crossed the line a few seconds later.

I had won!

Or so I thought.

"Humphrey! Humphrey! Humphrey!" the crowd cheered.

Mrs. Brisbane scooped me up and held me in her hand.

"Quiet, everyone!" Mr. Morales said.

Since he is the Most Important Person at Longfellow School, the crowd quieted down.

"Humphrey crossed the finish

line first," he said. "But he wasn't in his car. This was a hamster car race, so I think Winky is the winner."

"No!" I heard some students say.

"Winky was the first hamster to cross the line in his car," he said.

"But Humphrey was so smart," Golden-Miranda said. "He knew he was stuck and he still found a way to get to the finish line first."

Mr. Morales nodded. "That's true," he said. "And I'm proud of Humphrey. But I still think that Winky won."

"I have an idea," another voice said.

I knew that voice.

Aldo stepped forward. "What if we call it a tie?" he asked.

Mr. Morales thought for a moment. "We could do that," he said.

Suddenly everyone began to cheer. "Tie! Tie! Tie!"

Mr. Morales raised both hands to quiet them down. “All right,” he said. “I think we can call this a tie. Is that all right with you, Mandy?”

“They both did a great job,” Mandy said. “They just got to the line in different ways. So I think . . . it’s a tie!”

The cheering was so loud, it hurt my small hamster ears.

“Humphrey and Winky will each receive a first place certificate

*and* a box of Hamster Chew Chews from Pet-O-Rama," Mr. Morales said.

I LOVE-LOVE-LOVE Hamster Chew Chews.

The crowd got noisy again, but Mr. Morales raised his hands. "We have one more contest this afternoon," he said. "Longfellow School has two classroom frogs, so we're going to have a frog jumping contest."

"BOING-BOING-BOING!" I heard Og say.

The crowd cheered.

"George is the classroom pet in Mrs. Loomis's class," he said. "Og is the pet in Mrs. Brisbane's class. We're going to place them each at the starting line. The winner is the frog that jumps the farthest in one minute."

I remembered George! He was the reason that Og came to Room 26 in the first place.

George was in Mrs. Loomis's class already when she brought Og in. George is a huge bullfrog with a BIG-BIG-BIG voice. He didn't like Og and started making so much noise during class that Mrs. Loomis couldn't teach.

She gave Og to Room 26 and he's been here ever since.

"BOING-BOING-BOING!" Og shouted.

I could tell he was ready for the frog jumping contest.

Mrs. Loomis set George down on the starting line.

Mrs. Brisbane set Og down in his lane.

Og had a nice smile on his face.

George had a mean leer on his face.

And he was HUGE.

Could Og jump farther than a great, big bullfrog?

Mr. Morales said, "Remember, no one can touch the frogs, but you all can cheer. Now, ready, set, jump!"

Mrs. Loomis let go of George and Mrs. Brisbane let go of Og.

Nothing happened at first. George sat on the starting line and so did Og.

Suddenly, George took a giant leap forward.

The crowd cheered, but Og didn't budge.

"Go on, Og! You can win," I squeaked.

Og still didn't move.

"Go, Og, go!" the students chanted.

I was WORRIED-WORRIED-WORRIED until, suddenly, George let out a loud noise.

"RUM-RUM-RUM!" he bellowed in his deep voice.

And then Og did it!

He took a huge leap forward.

He leaped past George. Then he leaped again. And again!

"Go, Og, go! Go, Og, go!" the crowd cheered.

"Yay, Og!" I squeaked. "I knew you could do it."

I wasn't sure he heard me until

I heard him answer, "BOING-BOING-BOING-BOING!"

Even though everybody could see that Og had jumped the farthest, the students measured the distance.

"The winner is Og!" Mr. Morales said. "He will receive a jar of Froggy Fish Sticks from Pet-O-Rama."

Luckily, George didn't argue.

"BOING-BOING-BOING!" Og twanged.

"I want to thank you all for

our very first Racing Day," Mr. Morales said. "I think Longfellow School has the best classroom pets in the world."

"Yes!" I squeaked.

Winky and Og were GREAT-GREAT-GREAT pets.

I tried hard to be a great pet, too.

I'm not so sure about George.

Later that day, Mrs. Brisbane made an announcement. "This

week, I didn't assign a student to bring Humphrey home for the weekend," she said.

"Eeek!" I squeaked.

After all, I love going home with students on the weekend.

"Instead, I'm taking Humphrey and Og home with *me,*" she said. "They deserve a good rest."

I love going home with Mrs. Brisbane. I love it when Og can come, too.

The day had been full of surprises, but this was the best one of all.

"Doesn't that sound like fun, Og?" I squeaked to my friend.

"BOING-BOING-BOING-BOING-BOING!" he replied.

I knew exactly what he meant.